City Paddock

Also by Myra King and published by Ginninderra Press

The Journey of Velvet Brown

Myra King

City Paddock

Acknowledgements

'Cracked Glass Door', Shortlisted in the E.J. Brady (major section) (2007)

'Dust to Water', First prize, open section,
published by Deakin University Press (2008)

'My Brother Brannigan',
Commended in the Scarlet Stiletto Awards (2008)

'Where the Kookaburras Laugh', First Prize, UK Global Short Story

'Mind Games', published in *Eclecticism* (2008)

'Men-o-Stop', Finalist in Slippery When Wet competition (2008)

'Where the Truth Lies', Highly Commended,
JBWB short story comp (UK, 2009)

'The District Nurse Will Be Here Soon', published in *Islet* (2010)

City Paddock
ISBN 978 1 74027 629 0

First published 2010
Reprinted 2016

GINNINDERRA PRESS
PO Box 3461 Port Adelaide SA 5015
www.ginninderrapress.com.au

Contents

City Paddock

I've been watching grass grow. Every morning you can see me, an old bloke, on my way to the shops, lifting my feet carefully as I cross over a strip of it outlining a path. At first there were only grass seeds, scattered like salt in the earth. But when I started noticing the new grass grow a little more each day, I thought, How bloody sad am I?

I've stopped saying hello and avert my eyes when passing another footpath jockey. Too many knock-backs of the non-verbal kind. My g'day had gone to the wind once too often and when I stopped saying anything at all I knew I'd become like them. That's when I realised I needed to get back to where I came from.

The bucolic in me becomes more melancholic every passing day. I miss my old life. I miss the horses. I miss the early starts, the cold mornings at the track, the air breathing out of my lungs like frosted smoke.

I miss my mates and I miss my youth. And, worst of all, I don't feel any different. Of course I've slowed down a bit. But I know I could still show these young riders a thing or two about the game.

Horsemanship has become a dying art, just like me. Nearly finished my race but way behind the field. Eighty-two and put out to pasture like an old bloody horse left to neglect and the whim of the weather so the owners can say, 'Sure, I've still got Punters Pride. Couldn't let him go to the doggers. He's won us a lot of money over the years.'

Yeah, shoved out in the paddock of the forgotten. Same as me, only I got the city paddock. Its houses are hemmed in by fences of the private kind, to keep eyes from spying and feet from treading. Plants all identical – there must have been a sale on weeping mulberries at my local garden centre. Every bloody front yard in my street grows one like some bloody sad song.

Conforming to conformity, that's me. That old man who walks to the shop every day at the same time to buy his paper, more regular than your morning crap.

And as I walk home and pass over my strip of grass I wonder how many people do see me. The invisible, the untouchable, the unknown. Neighbours, but more distant than a foreign country. And none of them would ever guess what I am going to do this Sunday.

Kill Marguerite.

My mind will take me no further than this thought, this promise to myself. I can't see beyond this one deed I have been planning for less than a week.

Perhaps kill is too harsh a word. But it sounds quick and clean like I hope it will be. There is a word for a word which sounds like its meaning. But my schooling stopped with the war.

I'm not complaining; it's how I got started with the horses. And they became my life, more part of me than my own skin.

I was in the Light Horse, post Beersheba. I was with them too when they were disbanded in 1941.

Sad time for us when we were converted to a motor regiment. But we conformed and managed, and in a way I was glad our horses didn't have to suffer like those poor buggers did in the Great War. In the end, overwork, thirst and a bullet were all the rewards they got.

I joined up when I was only fifteen. Course I cheated on my age, lots of us did; no one insisted on birth certificates and such back then.

Old Jack Trentham took me under his wing. What he didn't know about horses wasn't worth remembering. He'd been dredged up from the Great War to teach us newcomers. We all thought we were crash hot. Most of us had come off farms and thought we knew it all. I was no different. And I wasn't a bad rider; well, you couldn't be no good and get in, you had to pass the test. Riding horses bareback over fences. Some of the horses were only newly broke too, and I remember watching several lads in front being dumped even before they got to the first jump.

I got lucky. The one I was given had some draught horse in him and he wasn't as spooky as the thoroughbred types. And his withers weren't as sharp. Some of the guys told me later they'd been nearly de-knackered on theirs.

I have only a few days to set the wheels of my plan in motion, literally. I don't own a car, only learnt to drive in my forties. Horses were my main transport up until then.

I check the telephone directory and find a place that hires cars out. I ring up and book one for the weekend. I haven't driven for over five years, the same length of time I've lived here, but I reckon it'll be just like riding a bike. That's all old Jack had for getting around after the war. Carrots, he called his bike. It was painted orange but had more paint missing than was left on it, although the rust matched, and you couldn't tell from a distance.

'Trouble with young folk these days, Bren, is they want too much,' he'd say. 'Too many things. Makes their lives too bloody complicated.'

That was one of the reasons I didn't get a car. Anyway, back then they cost more of your wage than they do now.

A few years after I got home from the front, my dad died and I inherited the farm.

I had two horses then, both broken to saddle and harness. I drove them in a cart up until 1966, when I got my first car, a Morris Series E. No starter motor, or at least not one that was worth trying. I didn't mind using the crank every morning. I just had to be careful when it kicked back. More cranky than any horse I ever owned.

Over the years there were other horses. Some thoroughbreds, which I trained and raced and had a few wins, and some foals I bred, but they were never any good. Not on the track anyway.

After lunch, I watch a programme about a new method of breaking in. Getting saddle and bridle on a horse and riding it in three hours flat.

I think about what Jack would have said. 'Young people have all the time but no patience, Bren. If a horse plays up, they want to get rid of it. They want results right now. Us oldies, our time is running out, but we know to take it slowly. Look for the cause, then you've got the cure.'

He was a damn good teacher, my old mate, Jack. Maybe I should have taken his advice in my marriage but when my wife played up I was too damn angry to be patient. Anyway, she left soon after I found out. I had no idea where she went and I didn't see my son until twelve years later when he was so grown up I nearly didn't recognise him.

After switching off the TV, I stare at the screen for several minutes, the black merging with my memories until I switch them off as well.

I go up to my room, unlock the cupboard, and slide out the drawer. Wrapped in an oil-stained cloth is my Bren gun. My companion in the war and the reason for my name. I smile to myself as I realise I've almost forgotten my real one; I haven't heard it for so long.

I rub the cloth over the barrel and stock. Pull it apart, check everything. Adjust the lever. The Bren isn't as stable when firing on automatic but I know it's rock-steady at single shot. I take out the box with the bullets. There are enough left. I didn't want to have to go to a gun shop and have them asking questions. Nowadays you have to have a licence to own a gun and I'm sure I wouldn't be allowed to keep a machine gun.

Just cause you have a licence, though, doesn't make you sensible. But I respect my Bren; I've seen what it can do.

Respect was high on Jack's agenda too. 'Always respect your horse,' he'd say. 'Remember that he's a hunted animal in the wild. The flight response is damn strong. And he's a bloody powerful beast. But gain his trust and respect and you'll have that strength working for you, not against you.'

My son, Paul, doesn't respect me. He never asks for my advice; pretty well does whatever he wants. He took me out to the farm last year; we hardly said a word all the way there. I was shocked to see how much it had gone down since I'd been packed off to the city. But the horses still looked good. Before I left, I'd teed it up with a neighbour, who has trotters, to keep an eye on them, rug them in winter, check they were getting enough feed and give them a regular worming. He had my number, with instructions to ring me if there was ever any trouble. I hadn't heard from him until last week.

I wrap some clothes around the gun and ammunition and pack them into a travel bag. Not that I think I may be searched but it pays to be careful.

I hadn't been careful enough that winter five years ago. I caught pneumonia, which put me into hospital and ultimately sent me to live in the city where I could receive 'help', as Paul calls it. Meals on wheels and a woman to come in once a fortnight to clean the floors and swish around the toilet with some disinfectant. 'You can do your own dusting,' she'd said. Bugger that for a joke; I'd never bothered with dusting before. A little dust never killed anyone. But a .303, well, that's another matter. The funny thing about war, though, is while it's happening you become desensitised. Easier to do if you don't get up close to your enemy. But those you come face to face with, well…you never forget.

'We're putting the farm on the market,' Paul said. 'It's not what we thought it would be like, living in the country. And Melanie misses the theatre and her old friends.'

What had they bloody well expected? Anyway, I wasn't really surprised. Actually, I was, but only that they'd stuck it out for five years. My cynical side told me it was probably because they were waiting for the market to go up, waiting for the rise in people seeking to be farm-charmed. Lately, I'd seen in the paper how country prices had boomed.

'Mel says we should take you on a nice holiday when we sell,' Paul said, his voice scratching through a lousy phone connection.

He didn't hear me enough to answer when I asked, 'What will you do with my horses?'

I look in the classifieds for what a Mitsubishi 380 looks like. That's the one I've hired. You don't get a choice. I've got a bit of an idea. I find out it's an automatic with power steering and cruise control.

Funny, you know: one of my horses had cruise control. You put him in a canter, dropped the reins on his neck, and he just kept at that pace until you picked them up again. Bloody lovely horse that one. Got snake-bitten. Stiff as the frost when I found him the next morning.

Jack always said you only get one or maybe two horses in your lifetime that are truly special to you. His was Goldie. My Goldie Pie, he called her. A Waler by breed, born in Australia but destined to die on foreign soil.

'Saddest day of my life, Bren, when I had to leave, knowing my Goldie Pie would soon be lying dead in the sand. I didn't envy the Vet Corps their job. And you know I can still hear her whickering out to me as we rowed back to the ship. Still, Bren, couldn't let the Turks have her. I mean, they're not bad people, bloody brave fighters and all that. But horses were just animals in every sense of the word to them. They would have worked her to death.'

A few days ago I got a phone call from Mel.

'Pa, I think I may have someone to take your mare,' she said. 'The local riding school is looking for another mount. When I told them about the mare they were really interested. They didn't even mind that she's so old. Safer for the inexperienced riders. Apparently they've been very busy with people travelling from the city to ride there every week. And the local schools have been running classes with them too. They have too much work and not enough horses.'

I'd caught my breath but she hadn't given me time to answer.

'You know we bought that place at Dover Gardens? We're moving there tomorrow. They could come and get her on Monday, they said. Trouble is, Pa, I can't catch her. She only trusts Sonia, but she's away at uni now. I was wondering if there was some way you could get out here.'

The line crackled but I could still hear her.

'Fucking country phone lines,' she said before the line went dead.

I think of Sonia, my granddaughter, how she was riding at three, fearless, or at least able to pit the fear and turn it back on itself. When was the last time I'd seen her?

Sunday comes up quickly. The only trouble I've had with the Mitsubishi has been oversteering as I was going out of the dealers. I managed to miss the gate, though.

I've got my gun and my mission, and on the long drive to the farm I find myself thinking about what I'm going to do. It's like my plan has been on one of those old records where the needle gets stuck and keeps repeating the one phrase, never going on with the rest of the song. But then something clicks it back on track and finally the tune can finish.

As soon as I got the phone call last week from my old neighbour, I knew there was something wrong.

'Which one?' I'd asked before he had time to speak.

'The gelding, Bren. He died overnight. I think he had colic. Ground was dug up and he had dirt all over him. Must have been rolling. Classic sign. I'm sorry. You know, he was nearly thirty. Bloody good innings for a horse.'

I'd felt guilt like lava churning my guts. 'He was tough, that one, he wouldn't have gone out quiet. How's the mare?'

'She's fretting, Bren. Running up and down the fence line. I've talked to Paul and Mel. They asked me to tell you what happened. They're going to see if someone with other horses will take her.'

We all call her the mare. But she has a name – well, two names, actually. Marguerite Miss Natural, her racing name; and Missy Mare, her stable name. Over the years it got shortened to Mare. I bred her twenty-five years ago. That makes her older than me in horse years. Four to our one. A centenarian.

The car seems to steer itself as we wind down familiar roads. I smile as I recall a yarn I heard at our local pub many years ago, of how old Jimmy was so drunk one night he could hardly stand up but they tied him onto his horse and slapped it on the rump. The horse took him home all right, but his missus left him strapped there until morning.

Now I can see Marguerite in the distance. She's calling out and pacing along the fence line like one of those tigers you see at the zoo. While I'm watching, she stops, strains her neck and neighs out once more. Then she spins around and gallops to the other end of the paddock. Even from here, I can see how much condition she's lost.

The farmhouse looks as sad as I feel. The windows have the shades pulled like closed eyes.

The hydrangea growing at the side droops, as despondent as the poppies before they bloom on the sand hills at Gallipoli. I breathe in the country air, can smell sheep and cows and horses. And the dry dust of the drought.

Marguerite comes over to me with remembrance in her brown eyes. They are eyes of trust, the same as those the soldiers would've looked into when they said goodbye on those distant shores so long ago. No way, Marguerite, are you going to end your days at the hands of others.

Her head is down as she follows me across the paddock. 'One last ride for us both,' I whisper, as I slide on her bridle. I lead her over to a fallen tree. Once, I could have sprung onto her back as easy as walking.

She strides out across the paddock then flows from a trot to a canter.

Afterwards, I slip from her back and take her over to my bag with its hidden promise.

I unwrap my Bren and load my two remaining bullets.

Cracked Glass Door

What if everything you have ever done and everything that has ever been done to you was to bring you to this point in your life? This apex, one you now summit to look out over unfamiliar mindscape crisscrossed with opportunities and living for the taking. How exciting to know all this could be formatted as completely as this story. And was even this preordained?

Fate. One word holding and withholding so much.

Your first remembered conscious thought flitting behind your eyes like tiny shadows. Tree leaves, sun tempered and a cool breeze which catches your breath from inexperience. Your babyness. The voice of your mother, with familiarity known from the beginning, and another harsher voice like wind on sea turning tempest. But you know nothing of storms and death and living. All you know is now and here and the warm sweet flow.

You feel empowered, not by thought but by reality of moment. You do this and this happens. You do more of this and the flow comes and you are changed and all is good. You have no words, not yet. But the power you have comes from your voice. You test it again and again and it does not fail you.

'I had to stick my tit in your mouth every time you cried,' your mother tells you. Age has deadened propriety and you cringe at her coarseness.

You know her mind is hardening, losing its ability. You wonder if this will be you in thirty years when you are eighty.

'Yes, your bloody father never let you cry. He would get so angry if you did. And you were always such a hungry little thing. But such a beautiful baby.' She pauses as if for effect. It works when she adds, 'I don't know if I could have loved you if you were an ugly baby.'

She continues after a long sip of her tea. 'I used to put you out under the cotoneaster tree and you would kick your little legs in the sunshine.' She moves her hands in simulation of your legs and you smile and nod.

You wonder at her memory; for a moment she seems normal and this conversation seems normal. Mother and daughter talking together. But not like old times, never like that. Then 'mother' was 'mum' and she never forgot your name.

You know the long-term memory is the last to go. And suddenly you want to know it all, want to understand this woman who gave you breath. It is a fascination not unlike summoning the afterlife and you know she will forget everything she has told you by the morning.

You listen and learn, hear about her brother molesting her when she was six and about the social worker who raped her when she was fourteen. You hear how she made all the clothes for her younger sisters, how she had a girls-only club and how she was always the leader. This surprises you, for it does not fit the template of the weak woman you have known all your life.

You see so much more just by her words. Her disclosure of the past.

'I had a lover once.' She leans forward, conspirator-like. 'He could fuck much better than your father.'

For a moment you feel jealous and an unknown trickle of something akin to loyalty runs down your psyche. Until you remember your hatred of your dad, and then it builds on the hill of discontent from being sired by such as he and sharing his genes forever. Why couldn't this lover be your father?

'What happened?' you say softly.

Your mother cups her ear.

'What happened? To your lover?' you add, wanting to make sure your mother stays on theme.

She doesn't answer the question but keeps on track. 'Thomas, his name was. My Tommy boy. He had five sisters, you know. I loved them all and they loved me.' She looks misty but perhaps it is only the cataracts.

She rubs knuckles, stretched smooth, across her eyes but you are still unsure.

'He loved me too, you know,' she says. 'My sister, April, told me that he was still asking about me right up until he died.'

You nod and hand her a hanky. She is crying but you feel strangely removed.

'He'd say to April, "Has she left that bastard yet?"'

You remember your Aunty April – all smiles and Country and Western. Your visits up north, the landscape as dry and cracked as an old man's foot. The air, suffocating with thick red dust, clutching your lungs. Your cousins laughing at your city words.

There is a silence. You wonder if your mother will go on. You will her with the thought and it seems to work.

'He came here once. All the way here. He lived up north, you know. Driving trucks.'

You try and picture your mother in the back of a truck with her lover. His face is a blur but he wears a blue singlet and shorts. You realise you are pigeonholing but you cannot stop. He has a blue heeler dog named Bitch and his truck is called Ramrod Betty or something equally as twee. There is a dice dangling from his rear view mirror and an Esky in the front seat, grimy with the grease from a thousand journeys.

You wonder if this fabrication is a remnant of the jealousy you felt earlier.

Your mother sits before you but she is far away.

Finally she speaks. 'He had a dog. I think he called it Bitty or something like that. No, no, it was Betty, the same as his truck. Black Betty, a Kenwood.' She sits upright with pleasure at the memory and her ability to bring it to voice. It seems to give her confidence to continue.

At the same time, you realise your recall is good too.

'You were there as well,' she says, confirming, 'but you were far too young to know what was happening.'

Suddenly your picture changes to two bodies entwined, gasping as if struggling for air. Your mother is moaning, Tommy, Tommy, Tommy over and over again. You are sure this is driven by imagination for they both look as old as your mother does now. You toss the thought away with a shake of your head and a turn of your stomach.

Your mother gets up and walks to the sink. Then she returns for the cups she should have taken with her. She carries them halfway, comes back and sits down again. She places one of the empty cups in front of you. 'What were we thinking about, dear?'

You grimace at the Freudian slip and for a moment you almost tell her. But instead you say, 'You were telling me about your lover, Tommy.'

'No,' she says. 'I wouldn't do that.'

Then she continues without acknowledging her denial. 'He wanted me to come back with him. Said he would leave his wife. Said I should get rid of the baby inside of me. He called it a little bastard. I think that's what stopped me. When he called my little one that.'

You knew your mother had miscarried once but you hadn't known when. You have only one older sister, Rachel. You quickly continue before she asks where the baby is.

'So what did you say?'

Your mother ignores your question. 'Then he said that I might lose it from what we had just done. You know…' She thrusts bent arms up and down, the gesture unmistakable.

You touch her shoulder and gently stop her. You are beyond embarrassment but it seems wrong to let her go on. You are suddenly glad this man is not your father after all. You much prefer your own dead one.

'Have you drunk your tea, dear?' She doesn't wait for your answer.

You get up and put the kettle on.

'Tommy loved coffee. Percolated. He bought me a percolator. I told your father it was a present from April.'

You remember the percolator and, like phoenix rising, there it is before you when you open the cupboard to fetch the tea canister. The brown glass is stained darker from the brewing. But you can't remember ever having coffee from it.

'He died, he did. My Tommy died it must have been two years ago. No, no, maybe it was ten years ago. Oh, I don't know any more.' She looks confused and shakes her head as if to level her thoughts.

You stir her tea and ask her how her sister, April, is. When last did she write?

Your mother rubs her eyes and looks to the side cabinet. The one that you remember from childhood; the one with the cracked glass door and cheap brown veneer. Nothing changes and yet everything has.

Your mother's voice alters clarity like a parting of clouds where the sun streams through, opening up blue sky, and you think the day won't be as bad as you first believed.

'I really loved him, I did. Tommy had the most beautiful voice. He could sing, you know. Baritone. I used to make him sing "Danny Boy" to me. He loved to sing that. His mother was Scottish. MacGregor her name was. Of course it wasn't Tommy's name. That was Brown. Just plain Brown.' Your mother laughs and finishes her tea.

'Sweetie,' she says, 'would you like a biscuit? I've bought some really nice ones. Not lousy old digestive biscuits like my stingy friend always gives me when I visit her.'

She goes over to the side cabinet and brings back some biscuits and a card with flowers on the front and 'Thinking of You' written in gold-embossed ink. 'And here, read this. It's from April. I got it on Friday.' She hands you the card and opens the biscuits.

You notice they are digestive ones. You read the letter from your Aunty April telling how the farm is in drought and how your cousins are struggling with mortgages and grown-up kids who won't leave home. And about your uncle Dennis, how his arthritis is so bad now he has to use a walker. Your aunty is well, though; she's still playing bowls.

'April sent me a letter when Tommy died,' your mother says. 'He was a widower by then. And he was still singing at the Returned Soldiers League right up until the last week.'

You try again to imagine him, this truck driving baritone lover of your mother. A thought rises unbidden. You wonder at his voice when he was making love, wonder if this was part of the attraction, the deep rutting of this man in love; or was it in lust? You choose the latter.

'Do you regret it, mother? Are you sorry you didn't go to him? I mean, you could have, after Dad died.'

'Could have what, dear?'

The clouds have closed again and you sigh at the darkness.

'You okay?' She looks worried for a moment but even concern does not last.

You begin to think that this may not be a bad thing, forgetting.

She seems to read your mind. And the clouds crack open to a slivered light. 'You know,' your mother says, 'I've been thinking that as we get older we lose everything so that it's easier when we have to go. Easier to give in. Nothing left to lose.' She continues, picking up the thread without prompting. 'Yes, I could have gone to him. My sweet Tommy. When we made love he was so gentle, so caring.'

You are not thinking about your mother's lover any more; you are thinking about the forgetting. Will she forget things she has never told you or anyone else, and then will they be as rhetorical as the tree falling in the forest? Does it mean they never happened?

Will she forget the sad and the angry times, the good and the bad equally, or will some memories remain stronger till the end for the position they held in her life?

'He had a huge cock,' your mother says. 'I think it might have been his Celtic blood.' She pronounces Celtic with a soft 'c'. And you wonder if she has always done this.

You desperately want to change the subject; your glance scurries across the room like a mouse. You walk over to the side cabinet and retrieve a book that is lying there.

'Mother, have you read this yet?' Your name is on the cover and the handwritten facsimile of it on the flyleaf along with the words 'To my mother with love'.

She takes the book from you and with an air of reverence she states, 'This is the book your sister Rachel wrote. She's a famous author now, you know.' She waves the book in your face.

You feel angry at the misplacing. 'Mother, I wrote this book. See, there's my name on the cover. And look, I even signed it for you.'

Your mother shakes her head, indifferent to your words and the irritation in your voice.

You suddenly chill with the realisation of another truth. Another memory. One many years ago, of your sister telling you about a man she had met with a dog called Betty and a big black truck.

And then you know without a doubt it was your older sister, Rachel, who was with your mother on that day. You were the one still inside her womb. Fate had stepped in before you were even born by the mother you had been given.

'Oh, Mum,' you whisper.

But now, again, she has turned away and does not hear.

Dust to Water

The great white egret
scans the landlocked lake and waits

I stand near the old pier, looking out over Lake Wendouree. There has been enough rain to make a difference – the lake is filling slowly and soon it will cover Edith Delaney's secret forever or for at least another lifetime. After all, the last time the lake dried up like this was in 1869 – fifty years before Edith was born.

My Aunt Beattie passed away early this year and she and Edith Delaney had been childhood friends, but I hadn't even known Edith existed until she phoned me soon after I posted the funeral notice. She couldn't make the service but when I told her I would be scattering Aunt Beattie's ashes on Lake Wendouree in several weeks time, she insisted on coming along. She'd heard about the Walk of a Lifetime event and how a safe path had been made across the lake. She agreed it would be a great time to carry out Beattie's last wish.

'We used to swim in the lake, you know, Andrea.'

I lift my eyebrows. 'Really?'

Edith takes a hanky from her sleeve and wipes her eyes. 'It was a lot cleaner then…' She surveys the 'Rocky Road' lakescape around us. 'I mean, that was seventy years ago. Everything was cleaner then.'

I smile and nod.

The lake bed looks like Edith's face on a grand scale. Sunburned. Cross-hatched dry from long years of drought. Crows' feet track the clotted mud, their owners with white wise eyes looking for easy pickings.

'Your Aunt Beattie was a great swimmer, lots better than I was.' Edith's hand trembles as she replaces her handkerchief. 'She could swim the length of the lake and stay underwater for ages. I could never do that. She would really scare me at times. I thought she had drowned.'

Instantly I have an image of Edith pacing the lake's shore like a trapped animal. Sunlight gilds the ripples made by paddle steamers and bric-a-brac boats into knife edges of light. I hear the whistle sounds of the steamers and of people laughing.

The fecundity of youth.

I open my eyes to the present.

'Do you want to stop and have a rest before we start across, Edith?'

The bus had been late and instead of waiting we had walked to the starting area.

I take her arm and lead her to the nearest bench.

'Everything changes, doesn't it?' she says.

We aren't looking at each other; our eyes are following the lines of people meandering across the lake like errant ants.

I know what she means. As you get older, mortality smacks you in the face with the number of people you have known who've died before their time. Before your time. Even those who die at ninety, like my Aunt Beattie, make you long for sameness or some sort of continuity.

She had lived a couple of blocks away and we'd been close all my life. I miss her terribly and it's only four weeks since she's been gone.

'Age is the great leveller, Andrea,' she had once said. 'Young people think we oldies were born old. But they find out. We all do.' And then, laughing, she'd added, 'It's just a matter of time.'

That's what I had loved most about her – her candidness. I guess that's why I was so surprised she hadn't told me about Edith Delaney.

We head out across the lake, people passing us quickly so those in front and those behind are never the same for more than a few moments.

'Did she ever marry, Andrea?'

I shake my head and look at the urn nestled in the crook of my arm. On my back I have a rucksack with bottles of water and a small foldaway stool just in case Edith needs another rest. It is two kilometres across and the going is not easy.

Edith stumbles on the soft turf and instinctively I grab her arm and hold her up.

'No one special then?' she says.

'No. She was in love with someone when she was young but she only told me his name. Eddie Montignac. And I only remember that because I asked her if the name was French. Montignac, that is, not Eddie.'

Edith breathes heavily; I stop, sling forward my rucksack, undo the zip and unfold the chair. With my bent elbow for support, Edith lowers herself onto it.

There is no break in the flow of people. We haven't reached the halfway point yet where a cameraman is taking photos. After that it is intermittent groups and stragglers.

I take the urn in both hands.

Edith shakes her head. 'No,' she mouths, 'not here.'

Her voice is barely a whisper and I am worried. I take out the water instead. Someone asks if everything is okay. My smile is twisted as I say yes.

'Let's head back.'

Edith straightens. 'No,' she says, her voice much stronger. 'I want to see it just one more time.' She gets up from the stool and stands looking ahead.

'See what?'

She doesn't answer but keeps staring into the distance. I can see the other side more clearly now. Someone is handing out certificates. For no real reason, I want one. A quote comes to mind: 'Awards are like haemorrhoids, eventually every arsehole gets one.' Strangely I don't feel like laughing.

'Are you sure you'll be all right?'

But already she is walking and by the time I pack away the stool and water bottles I have to run to catch up.

'You've been married, though, Edith, haven't you? You said you had a daughter.'

'Yes, she lives in Queensland. I go up every year to see her. Get away from the cold.'

We pass a discarded sandal. We both glance at it. Post-drought. Dropped there when the strap broke. No more use to its wearer. No historic worth. Funny how we value antique things but not antique people.

We reach the end. Stewards are giving out papers; they congratulate us. I look at Edith but she is not smiling. And I still have not done what I came for.

Irritation flickers a frown and Edith looks at me worriedly.

Now it is she who takes me by the arm and we stroll along the path until we are away from the throng.

'I want to show you something.'

The sun glances her face, smoothing the lines with light or perhaps the brightness blinds me as just for a moment she looks young.

'I know where Beattie would want to be. It's still here. I saw it the other day.'

Now she strides ahead. She climbs down a small embankment. Willow trees encircle us. We can see no one through their low hanging branches.

'Be careful. The ground is slippery,' I say as I skid down to join her.

She is pointing to a single pylon. 'The old pier. This is where your Aunt Beattie and I would go swimming. I was always too scared to put my head under water. I think that's why she was faster. Look.' She points, grim reaper like.

I follow the line of her thin finger and see, etched in the wood below the water line, a faint heart with initials. I move closer.

'I never got to see it until the other day,' she says. 'Beattie scratched that there seventy years ago. Before I left for college. Before our friendship ended.' Tears stream down her face. 'The water kept it hidden. I mean, it was unheard of in those days. Beattie was older than me. She was the one who ended it. I was only eighteen. And she knew I wanted to have children.'

Edith slides forward; I grab for her and drop the urn. Some of Beattie's ashes mix with the small trickle of water flowing there. I pour out the rest and we watch as they float on the surface and swirl as gentle as a fingertip caress, around the bottom of the pylon.

'Edith…?'

'Some people call me Eddie,' she says.

My Brother Brannigan

My brother, Brannigan, flicks a small wad of paper at Pythagoras, my cat, and then looks at me. I know what that look means: I feel like an argument, and I really hope you're gonna bite.

'You know, Rosie, God's already invented perpetual motion.'

Pythagoras hardly moves, merely shivers out a foot like someone testing the water and opens hostile-looking eyes in Brannigan's direction. He usually keeps that look for me.

I hope I appear at least as disdainful.

I'd only agreed to let Brannigan stay at my house until he got on his feet. But it seems for the past year he's hardly got off his chair. The one that used to be Pythagoras's exclusive perch. My cat loves being atop things, never sits *in* your lap or *on* a chair. Like a judge on high, Pythagoras always perches.

'Are you speaking about the tides?' I say, lifting my fingers from my keyboard. 'And anyway, it all depends on how far you take perpetual. I mean, everything has an end. Even the earth will cease one day. You know, when the sun turns Nova.'

Oh shit, I think to myself. Is that what it's called? I don't want to lose the argument before it's begun. I click Thesaurus, glad that my computer is facing away from Brannigan, and I'm gladder still when I discover I'm right.

Brannigan leans forward. He squints like he's trying to exude some facts from his brain. For a few seconds, mental constipation seems to rule. He clears his throat. 'Well, Sis, not just the tides, and if you insist on playing semantics then nothing is perpetual.' He rubs his forehead then continues. 'What about the planets' rotation around the sun? And the earth spinning on its axis? How does that song from Monty Python's *Meaning of Life* go again?' He starts to hum, 'The world is spinning round at…' His voice fades out like an old-time movie.

Brannigan is not my brother's real name. He adopted it from a character in *Futurama*, a cartoon series. Personally I couldn't think of a worse namesake. The original is an overbearing arsehole. And I'm being kind.

Brannigan did have a job working for the council on the emergency crew, cleaning up after storms and such, but he threw it in for a sea change. Not an investment in beach property but in a luxury cruise boat. Two months later when it mysteriously caught fire, Brannigan found out there was no insurance, so he and five other investors went down with the ship. Then he was so much in debt he couldn't afford to pay his rent.

Pythagoras mews to be let out, thereby saving me from biting a chunk off what probably is the real issue: the fact Brannigan had said 'God'. Anyone who knows my brother knows he is an atheist of the dyed-in-the-evolution kind. He would've expected me to say something about the reference.

I watch Pythagoras walk across the dusk-dampened grass, mincing with his front paws as if he's counting the prints. Then I shut the door and turn around to survey the planet that is my brother. Starting at his head, I notice the undergrowth of grey hair pushing forward a frown. His hands fondle the remote control like a lover and his long body towers above his legs, supported by the footrest of the recliner.

Dr Phil, the TV psychologist, springs to life in the corner. The topic for today's show is Moochers. The word screams across the screen like a foregone conclusion. I find myself standing and watching.

'You're disempowering your adult son, Mrs Hogswallop, by keeping him home with you,' Dr Phil says, in his indomitable Texas drawl. 'You're not helping him at all. And all because of your own guilt. For not being the mother you think you oughta have been while he was growing up.'

I grip the back of Brannigan's chair and bite my lower lip. I really should be getting back to my thesis. Girls versus boys, in mathematics and science.

I'm a maths teacher. I've always loved numbers. They have a reliability and solidarity to them. Rules in maths don't change like they do in life. A measure is a measure and a number is a number.

I never had any kids of my own. I got all mothered out bringing up Brannigan while our parents played drug dealers in our little home town of Malbacca. They ended up taking more than making and we became orphans before I was eighteen and Brannigan was nine.

I remember the dark blind of my bedroom, the tiny pins of light pricking through a myriad of holes. I would count them every morning when the sun shone. I'd only feel good for the day if I reached five hundred. Many a time my parents would break the tally with their fighting and I would rush to my brother's room to calm his fear, while mine grew as rampant as the weeds in our backyard.

Everyone in Malbacca was sure we'd turn out bad like our folks so I got Brannigan away from there soon after we buried our mother.

'Branny, can you please turn that down? You know I have to have silence when I'm working. School goes back next week. I still have lots to do.'

'What's that, Sis? I can't hear you. The TV's going.' He slips me a sideways grin and then, as he sees me beginning to overarm a paperweight in his direction, holds up the remote control in a gesture of truce. 'Okay, okay, I'm doing it.'

I'll be turning forty next year; Brannigan has just started his thirties. My grandmother used to tell me that's when men's brains mature. Perhaps his will ripen soon. One can only hope.

'You know, Rosie,' Brannigan says, clicking the remote control at the TV like a gun and swivelling around to face me, 'I was referring to you before when I said about perpetual motion.'

I raise eyebrows as the TV screen blanks to black. 'What the hell are you talking about now? Honestly, Brannigan, the sooner you get back to work, find your own place and get that bloody log off your shoulder the better.' Oh God, I sound like our mother should have sounded.

'Rosie, Rosie, Rosie. You can't help it, can you? Hold onto your teacher's desk-side manner for a moment, will you. All I meant was, you never stop working. You're perpetual motion personified. You know, it doesn't hurt to slow down sometimes.'

I take a deep breath. But Brannigan is heading off before the wind of indignation fans the words sparking my synapses like a firing squad. Before the first syllable reaches my lips, he's out of the door, cross-jumping over Pythagoras who has taken this opportunity to come back inside.

Lately, Brannigan's been running hot and cold like a faulty tap, sometimes annoying and argumentative, but at other times it's like he's caught the happiness bug. As I'm scanning these thoughts I gasp back a revelation. Could he be taking drugs? Our mother used to be like this.

Not that she was any better when she was high; she'd still lie around the house while I prepared meals and picked up the detritus of her and dad's drug revelries. The only thing different was she wouldn't be throwing things at me or taking the electric cord to Brannigan. And she never gave us encouragement or listened to us.

It's now I remember that, about a week ago, Brannigan had wanted to talk to me about something. I was heading out of the door to go food shopping when he'd asked, so I'd fobbed him off, told him we'd chat later. But Brannigan was gone when I got back. Was he going to tell me he'd been bitten by the drug monkey?

I scribble some numbers on a spare piece of paper, tally them up, then multiply them and divide them to the nearest decimal. I feel calmness returning like a slow tide.

The front door opens and, using it as a shield, Brannigan sticks his head around. 'Safe to come back, Sis? Requesting permission to come on board, or should that be in board?'

I'm standing now. I must be looking strange because after Brannigan re-enters he stops and stares at me. Before he can ask, I sit down on the couch and pat the seat next to me.

'Sit, Branny. I'm ready to talk now.'

He lifts shaggy brows. It seems like he's about to say something but his mouth opens then shuts, closing any words.

'Remember last Sunday when I went shopping, Bran? You wanted to tell me something? But you weren't here when I got back.'

'Yeah, well, Rosie. I had people to see. You know.'

'Oh, god, Branny, just tell me you haven't got involved in the drug scene.'

'Okay. I haven't got involved in the drug scene. Is that what you want to hear?' His eyes narrow in my direction before he drops his gaze to the floor.

Words come in a rush but clog my throat trying to escape.

'Rosie, you're just like all those people at Malbacca. You must have been real happy when my venture failed. Proved you and them right.'

I find my voice but it's only a whisper. 'That's not true, Bran. How can you say that? I've always done the best for you.' Inwardly I'm thinking, oh, Branny, if you only knew.

I used to think my mother was worse than my father, until I discovered what Dad had been doing to Brannigan. It was my end of year exams and I had been up late studying when I heard Brannigan crying. I rushed to his room, found his bed a tangle of blankets and sheets, and I spent several minutes wrestling the covers from him. All the while, I was asking Brannigan what was the matter, what had happened, and reassuring him that it was me, his sister, Rosie. When I finally saw his face, I wished I hadn't. And when I saw the blood, I knew.

It was no use confronting my father with the truth that night, nothing could wake him. But the next morning I faced him with all the fury that my seventeen years of hell could hold. I told him I was going to the police. In the end he came up with his own sentence.

The ratio of length of rope to body weight and height of drop has to be precise if the action is not to result in decapitation or strangulation. Dad was lucky; he had a daughter who topped her class in maths. There are numbers to everything if you look.

I lean over and hug Brannigan to me like a child. 'I knew you wouldn't go down that road, Bran. But just tell me what's up. Talk to me.'

Bran pulls away. His body stiffens. 'I've never told anyone this before,

Rosie.' Bran stares down at his hands clasping his knees. 'I was there in the room when Mum died. I watched it happen. And you know what? I didn't give a damn. My own mother and all I felt was relief. I didn't even go for help. What sort of monster does that make me?'

'She was my mother too,' I say, my voice barely grazing my breath.

Bran looks at me with wide eyes, like I've just uttered a revelation. Then he glares over my shoulder to a point of unfocus.

'You know how I went after Mum and Dad died? How I started denigrating religion? I wasn't being honest with myself, Sis. I do believe in God. I never really stopped. I just couldn't face what I'd become.' Brannigan runs open fingers backwards through his hair, starts to get up then slumps down in his chair again. 'That's where I've been going, Rosie, I've met this group. Don't worry, I know what I'm doing. It's not a cult. They're wonderful people. I feel great when I'm with them.'

Now it was my turn for the revelation look. I wasn't expecting this. Then I remember how much Brannigan had loved Sunday school when he was little.

I was the one who found Dad. I made sure of that.

I cried at his funeral but only for what could have been, not for what was. Brannigan didn't shed a tear. But he changed after we moved. He didn't go real bad, just got into fights and started shoplifting.

When he was in his early twenties, he deed-polled his name to Brannigan.

Pythagoras makes a short mew and leaps onto my lap. He has the 'pat me now' look.

I stroke his thick fur, he arches his back against my hand and I feel his Geiger counter purring through my fingertips.

'Rosie, my friends at church told me that if I confess to whatever I've done and ask for forgiveness, God will understand. I'll be clean. Maybe my life will patch up too. You know, I've never felt worthy of anything good happening to me. I might seem jealous of you sometimes, but I'm not. You deserve all the good things.' Brannigan waves his hand around the room and I follow it.

My look casts over the plasma screen TV, the leather lounge suite, the woollen rugs. Hardly opulent, but I've done okay.

Brannigan leans forward. 'The other stuff I've done, there's no problem confessing to that. But how can I tell them what Dad was doing? I'm so ashamed. It was happening long before you found out. Soon after my seventh birthday. And the thing is…' Brannigan straightens up, looks at me like a direct challenge and continues. 'The thing is, Mum knew about it, Rosie. She knew what Dad was doing to me and she never tried to stop him.'

I wasn't surprised. When I'd confronted Dad, Mum had stood by as silent as mist. I hated her more in that moment then I ever did our father.

I push Pythagoras off my lap and take Brannigan's hand. 'Don't you dare feel guilty, Branny. You did nothing wrong and, if anything, you deserve good things more than I do.' I squeeze his fingers. 'And if your church doesn't understand, then all I can say is to hell with it. You're better off without them.'

'I do feel guilty, though, Sis. Like I said, I watched Mum die. Watched as her breathing became slower and slower, until her chest didn't rise any more. I was pleased she was gone. And Rosie, I don't think I feel sorry about it, even now. That's why I get so angry at times. Even after she's gone I can't get any peace.'

'Well, Bran, confess this to whoever it is you believe in. No one else need know.'

For several minutes we sit hand in hand. Still and quiet.

Then Bran gets up, pulling me with him, and says, 'I'll do that, Rosie. I'll ask God to build up my faith. Help me feel repentant. That will work. I know it will. It has to.' Bran squeezes my fingers, his look softens.

But I feel my face creasing a frown. I need to keep my thoughts moving. I need to be doing something. Before I can stop them I hear the echoed words from the night our mother overdosed.

'Can you get me my fix, Rosie? There's a good girl. You know how much I have. Don't forget to boil it well and good. The spoon's on the sink. You'll find a syringe in the medicine cabinet. Use the one with measurements along the side.' And, when I'd hesitated, her voice as strident as death: 'Come on, you worthless little slut. Can't you see I'm suffering? I've just lost my husband, for Christ's sake.'

Now I see the picture of me mixing, measuring and then measuring some more. I hadn't thought about Brannigan finding her. If I had, I would have locked him in his room until I was sure it was over.

From the top of my chair, Pythagoras's golden eyes peer at me as clear as judgement, but I meet their stare and hold it. Then he turns his head away and drops down from his perch.

Returning to my computer, I begin to type. I lean back, exhale a long breath and feel myself and my thoughts slink away to a darker part of tomorrow.

Where the Kookaburras Laugh

There's a different feel to the air in the cemetery when the evening cools and calls. A cloistered breeze touches the stones, wafts across the fenced-in plots of blood-rust steel and bone-coloured cement. Somewhere near, a crow caws its bawdy ballad, the last note a drawn lament. But the kookaburras too have their song.

A little boy, Danny, walks alone along the rows, stopping in front of one particular gravestone where the inscription has eroded to undecipherable scratches. His head moves from side to side, his lips soundless, mouthing words that cannot be read.

Danny lives nearby with his mam, his gran and his uncle, the brother of his father who died in the Great War. Danny's mam got the telegram the day Danny was born. For her, his father died in childbirth.

Danny stoops and stretches an arm as pale as a robber's promise through the steel pikes, feels the rust rub his skin, leave a mark like ochre. Like warpaint.

His fingers touch the top of an imbedded flower container. There is an earthen ping, then his treasure (a small lead horse, hand-painted and unmounted by harness or rider) becomes as irretrievable as rain.

'Danny, lad, where are you, boy?' His uncle's voice seems not to echo here.

Danny doesn't answer but crouches at the side of the grave. He listens as the sound descends on him with the impending dark.

'There you are. What are you doing?'

'Nothing, Uncle Don.'

'Well, get up, lad, and dust yourself off. Your mam's had your dinner ready for an hour now. She's fit to burst. Come along, quick.' His uncle turns round and heads off without waiting.

Danny pulls himself up using the grave-fence for support, rubs rust-powdered hands over his knees and the tops of his shorts. He smiles, strangely satisfied at the result. He puts his hand in his pocket, feels the carrot nestled there like a fifth finger, and quickens his pace.

The moon is up already, even though the sun has just sat down on the horizon. The cemetery seems to breathe Danny gone, trails behind him so that he is too scared to look back.

He stumbles on the rocky track that leads back to his house. Ghost gum branches spider-web the evening sky, ensnare the light but speed his step. Soon he is at the horse paddock and Major, their carthorse, snickers softly, an almost human sound. Danny hears the horse before he comes into dusk-focus, grey silhouette on grey, the familiar smell of horse sweat and dirt as comforting as a hug.

Soft but bristled lips nuzzle his hand; he opens it, keeping the palm flat, and the carrot is whisked away in a disappearing act. There are sounds of crunching, then the big head comes back, nose tucks under Danny's empty hand and flicks it upwards.

'Hey, Major. There's no more, boy.' Danny laughs as the horse quivers back his lips, white teeth visible in the moonshine, almost a smile.

He climbs up the fence and slips a leg over Major's broad back. Major shakes his head as if in mock amusement and begins to amble back towards the farmhouse, his footfalls cuffing his huge feet in dust haloes.

Sliding from Major's back, Danny stands staring at his home. It looks oddly like the cemetery in this light. The fence of steel and picket demarcates the house from paddock and track. The front door is shut, the black form of the knocker hangs there like a decaying tooth.

The door opens; he sees his mam, hand shading her eyes as if scanning the sun. She stares at him, sight unseeing. He comes forward into the thin light streaming about her.

Her hand, as fast as a snake, snatches him to her side. 'Where have you been? And look at the state you're in.'

Rough fingers streak down his front and the blood-rust is smeared. He notices her hands are wearing it now.

There is a gust of wind, Danny shivers, sees his uncle standing behind his mam with the horse whip held upright. His eyes look tired but his grip is firm.

'I'm sorry, my lad, but your mam is right. You can't keep going off when it's getting dark. It worries her. And it pains me to be the one to have to put it right.'

Major neighs for his dinner, the noise follows Danny into the house but the door is shut behind him and the sound is cut mute. We'll both go hungry tonight, he thinks, but at least Major will miss out on the flogging.

Some time later, Danny hears a soft tap on his bedroom door; he rolls over from his stomach and sits up slowly. The door opens and Gran Sarah, his father's mother, creeps bent to his bed, balanced by a candle in one hand and a plate of sandwiches in the other.

'Hush there now, lad. I couldn't be letting you go without supper. Eat quiet like and slip the plate under the bed when you're finished with it. I'll collect it myself in the morning.'

'Why does me mam hate me so, Gran?'

'Ah, she's always been under a drop that one, never bonnie like your Aunt Rosie. And like I've said before, lad, when she got the news of your da, in the midst of her birthing, she tied the blame to you. I don't think she understands it herself but there it is and no denying.'

Danny takes the plate. The gloom has parted slightly and he watches as his gran shuffles on leaden feet from the room. He lies back on the bed but sleep darts from behind his lids. Images and voices of snatched conversations are caught in his mind: *selling up…moving…*

Danny has lived here all his life. His gran came from Ireland sixty years ago when she was just a lass and freshly wed. And when Danny's grandpa died, his mam and his da moved in to help his uncle Don run the farm. After the war ended, it began receding year by year, fifty acres sold off here, ten there, until now there is just the oasis of the horse paddock left. The working dogs are growing lazy and Major only has the cart to pull, the horse-drawn harvester has gone the way of the stump-jump plough. Sold to the highest bidder at their farm auction two weeks ago.

Danny's mam ignores him when he comes for breakfast the next morning.

She's talking to his uncle Don, her voice as light as a thread. 'So, you did order the green one? The one I saw advertised in the catalogue?'

Uncle Don tousles Danny's hair, last night's beating forgotten with the dawn. 'Just like a woman,' he says. 'To be worrying about an incidental thing like a colour. I know what you want to hear, Danny. Ah, my lad, it truly is a wonderful thing to see. A Buick – a touring car. All six cylinders, four-speed gearbox and rear-wheel drive of her. Dozens of horses under her bonnet. Makes a mockery of old Major out there.' He cocks his thumb towards the paddock.

Danny is pleased to see someone has fed the horse. Major stands in a circle of hay. Strands of golden raffia cascade from his mouth and reflect the silver in his coat. He snorts the dust and stomps the flies. It seems to Danny that the earth tremors beneath those hooves. No car could ever match that.

His mam scoops tea leaves from the Bushells tea caddy. Danny can see the kangaroo and koala, soft grey embossed. He tries to find the kookaburra but the tin is facing the wrong way.

'Should be a treat to drive on the good roads when we move back to town,' his mam says.

Danny's gran is in one of her talking moods. She sits, perpetually cold despite the weather, in her favourite chair, with a rug over her knees. She only has Danny for an audience. But his ears are as forward as old Major's are when the dogs are howling at the moon.

'I just wish I had my boy back here in the place where he was birthed. Not buried in some far-flung country which I can never visit. I think it would have helped your mam too, Danny. Although I still have my Don. Nothing like my Adrian, though, but I'd never say it to him. Your da loved horses, like you. He had no time for the automobiles.'

Danny sits closer, plucks at a stray thread on the side of the old chair, feels it flake and disintegrate beneath his fingers. 'I have somewhere I go to visit my da.'

His voice is low and his gran cups her ear and leans towards him.

'I have somewhere I go,' he says, so loudly that she withdraws as if she's been shot.

'No need to yell, boy. I'm not deaf. What's that? You have someone you know?'

Danny folds his arms around his legs, drawing them close to his chest. He rests his chin in the dip between his knees. 'Tell me again. About my da,' he says.

Later, with her story still sounding in his mind, Danny leaves his sleeping gran and runs to the horse paddock.

Major sees the bridle he's carrying and skitters away like a colt. But then he stops, wheels around, takes a few steps towards Danny and lowers his head. Danny approaches slowly, all soft-voiced words and promised treats. He slips on the bridle and fastens the strap. With thin strong hands he grabs a hunk of mane at the horse's withers and as deftly as a jockey, vaults onto his back.

'Go!' He screams it like a battle cry.

Major accelerates, his large bulk a catapult, but Danny is ready. He leans forward along the horse's neck, his bare heels batter Major's sides like tiny fists. He can feel his own heart and the strong pulse of living force beneath him. All around, those of the Fourth Light Horse Regiment are galloping in a mad headlong dash, some to oblivion, some to live to die another day. The horses by the hands of the ones they trusted. Can't let the Turks have them.

He whispers in Major's ear; it flickers back, listening.

'We can do it this time, boy.'

Danny sees the fence approaching, sees the top wire, a tightrope of tiny razors stringing across it. 'To the wells of Beersheba,' he yells.

The fence is in front of them, larger now by its closeness.

'Over!'

The one word like a spur. He digs in his heels, loosens the reins and lifts with the leap. For one suspended moment both are flying.

'We've done it, boy! We've jumped the trenches. We've saved the troops.'

Danny lets the horse stretch out under him, feels the smoothness of the gallop, watches over Major's shoulder for pitfalls in the unravelling terrain. Moves his hands, steers him safe. Horse and rider saving each other. His breath gasps and grasps his chest. He smells the acridity of fear and death. He hears the battle, the shots, the screams, the thuds of fallen men and horses. Knows his father is one amongst them. Danny lets out his breath, a long sigh that seems like it will never end.

Soon he reins Major to slow, loosens his grip once more as the graveyard comes into focus. It is different in the daylight. He only goes there in the dark. In the light it would be too hard to pretend. He thinks of his father, of the gravestone with the make-believe words, thinks of the little lead horse, of town, wonders if the kookaburras will laugh there.

Mind Games

10 April 2037

Rendine Philips polishes his courage and enters the fray. Not virtual reality, more reality virtuous. He feels the pull and the push. Electricity pulses resistance.

He finds it hard to believe that here he is – he, Rendine – playing mind games with Fergus Holinger. The best. And so many watching. He can feel their thoughts distracting, disconnecting his concentration.

He sees the vortex, Fergus's mind, although he's still tangled to his own. Tenuous thread. Eyelids flicker REM. But this is no ordinary sleep. Not made for resting. Made to test mental metal. The power of the mind in real time. His against the other.

There are mind-words before him, ones he doesn't have to read, ones he feels through thoughts. Familiar echoes of many times with other minds, before Fergus. But these are so clear he bends back. Listens.

Come, Rendine, I need to pressure you to focus. I can already feel you.

Rendine tries to answer, cannot. Sees the inner workings, thinks, My mind must look like this.

Yes.

Blanched, black and red. A hollow spiral without end. Gaps of light dart like a torch flashed at the night sky. A glimpse of the 'I' that is Fergus.

Yes, come. The first round has begun.

Rendine tries to tie his thoughts to memory. Moves like a bishop. Diagonally. Fails to think back, is here, now. Only in this second, and then this one, on and on.

The moment is the past as soon as he thinks of it. He tries to hold it, harness it to now, invert it so it has no beginning, no end.

Tell me how you can do that. How can you be in the moment? Tell me the story.

A circle?

Too easy, Rendine.

I need time.

Yes.

A man is gasping, he looks to the ceiling of his room and feels his time is short…

Yes, go on.

The man lets out a sigh. The moment of death has no past or future, only the present.

Yes. Good.

Rendine's turn. He asks but does not ask, A question which is not a question? Tell me the story, Fergus.

A statement.

Too easy, Fergus. Tell me the story.

A man named Rendine wants to prove himself. He goes to the Mind Games. Tries for years. Has some wins and some losses. Time goes on and technology improves. Finds ways of disengaging mind from body. It is nothing new. Many people have learned the art. Science finds a way to do it on demand. Then learns to merge the minds. The games become cerebral. No way of bluffing. Questions are felt, not told. Shown not asked. A question but not a question.

Tension drops. Rendine floats on the half-time interval. A quiet light in a stream, like a billowing sail.

No time seems to have passed at all when Rendine feels Fergus's words.

Round two begins now, Rendine. Are you ready?

Fear suddenly clenches him like a fist. Tight, suffocating. He tries to fight it. Wants to get away.

Tell me, Rendine, how you can do that. How can you escape? Tell me the story.

A little girl is frightened of a bully. Every morning he punches her and takes her lunch money. She gets so scared she cannot sleep at night. Doesn't want to go to school. One day she faces him and tells him to stop. He hits her and she falls down and skins her knee. The pain is so bad she gets cross and, arms flailing, she runs screaming at the bully. He turns away and skitters off.

Fear has taught its lesson to be brave. Bravery is never defined by non-existence of fear. It needs the contrast of it to kick back against, to test the fire of courage. Fire that will destroy or strengthen.

No escape necessary. Fear becomes the coward when confronted.

Mm. Now challenge me.

Rendine sends mind-words like email: a man running over his three-year-old child in his four-wheel drive. Should have bought a reversing camera. Opted not to. Guilt, avalanche of heaviness. Tell me how he can survive this. How can he live with this guilt? Tell me the story.

A moment passes. Rendine waits. Knows this will add to his points.

Tell me the story, Fergus.

The man is fixing the tow bar, crouching low behind the car. The child gets into the car without him knowing, slips behind the wheel. She is playing, releases the handbrake. The man is crushed, taken to hospital. While he lies dying, he tells his daughter that he does not blame her. It was an accident. Reverse the incident and forgive yourself as you would have forgiven them.

Light flickers consciousness. Rendine is returning, feels his body being slipped on like a glove. Opens his eyes to the operations room. Brings back the recall. Remembers lying down here – how long ago? Glances at the clock on the glass wall and sees the people behind it. Some rising to leave. Some opening their lunch boxes. Some still writing notes.

He sees that two hours has passed. Smells the remnants of the Chloether in the back of his throat. Strong, pungent. Aroma pathway to another's mind.

'Back with us, then?' Angela, gold warm, with eyes of concern.

'You should see the other bloke.' Ancient joke, feels silly as soon as he's uttered it.

Angela takes his wrist. 'I have,' she says, counting. 'You did good, Ren. First time with the Master. I'm impressed. High score on round two, I think.'

Rendine waves his hand around the circular room. 'The Gallery. What did they think? They're the ones voting.'

'Find out soon enough. See if they want more. Stats are okay. You could go another four rounds.'

Rendine slumps on the stretcher. Angela releases the straps which are holding him in. He drops his arms to the void on either side. Clenches and unclenches his hands, shakes his fingers. Starts to sit up. Feels the blackness swirling, not unpleasant. Slumps down again. Remembers that it takes a few minutes to knit the mind to the flesh.

Angela is frowning. 'Take it easy, Ren. Rest a few minutes. Then I'll take you up on that lunch offer.'

Rendine starts to say he hasn't asked her. Bites off the words with a grin. 'Right,' he says. When he takes Angela's arm he feels euphoric, one of the side effects of Chloether. Not a bad one, he thinks. The side effect and Angela.

'What are you grinning about, Ren?'

Rendine touches her arm, 'You, amongst other things,' he says.

'What?' she laughs. 'Like sheets?'

The campus's vastness requires the air-o-bus to carry them across. The cafeteria that Angela has chosen is on the north side.

They both wear their micromobs: the ring that rings. Rendine's mind plays back the slogan that made them so popular. Two years after they were launched, hand-held mobiles became obsolete. His is glowing azure blue, signalling that it is on and fully charged.

The café offers the usual fare. Organic modified. Natural modified. Plain predate.

Angela stares at the menu. 'I can never tell the difference. Even now that they have these smile stickers.' She stops and turns to Rendine. 'What do three smiles mean again?'

'Buggered if I know. Must be better. Stands to reason.'

Memories of his childhood. Happy Meals. Had to be thirty years since he'd had one of those. Not long before the greatest lawsuit in history sent McDonalds to hamburger heaven.

This is turning into a great afternoon, Rendine thinks. He can't remember ever chatting up Angela before. It seemed like she was way out of his league. Even if he didn't win the game, having this 'happy meal' with Angela would make it all worthwhile.

'Hey, Ange,' he says. 'Look over there, isn't that…

'Yes, it is. It's Fergus. Don't, Ren. It's against the rules to engage with the opponent before a decision has been made.'

'I know that. But he's looking at us.'

The sky surrounds Rendine with its usual cloudless grey as he waits on the glass platform. He can hear the gentle whoosh of the wind converters charging the generators. The temperature is constant. Twenty-one degrees.

His micromob has been silent. No news is good news perhaps, he thinks. Angie has returned home; her shift had finished with round two.

So, we meet in the flesh.

Rendine whirls around. Sees Fergus standing back, behind two students both busy talking on their micromobs.

They stare at each other. Know the inner working of each other's minds. Feel that not even sex is as intimate. They still have the ability to think in unison. No change of point of view necessary. Another side effect of Chloether, Rendine thinks.

Yes, says Fergus. But his mouth is closed.

Has the Gallery decided? Rendine tries to read his mind.

Blankness. Like the look on Fergus's face.

Come with me.

Solid walls abut either side of the sentence.

Rendine finds his legs moving. Feet follow in step with Fergus. Feels like he is in a dream. They climb onto the air-o-bus together. Sit together. For a moment Rendine hears only his own thoughts. Doesn't feel like probing. Feels like sleeping.

The bus is creating tides of wind. Started twenty years ago with the first sucking in of air turning the turbines. And going on ever since. In and out. This friction causes gravity absorbing vibration, making perpetual motion possible. The air-o-bus never shuts down.

Rendine wonders why Fergus is telling him things he already knows. Anyway, he thinks, it's not that simple.

He doesn't know where they are going but he knows it's not back to the operations room.

Now he is walking behind Fergus. Not caring, just wanting to stop and rest his eyes.

A building looms closer, towering like a giant leaning down to touch them.

Rendine shakes his head and the building stands upright again. He realises he's still on campus. These are the lecturers' quarters. Fergus territory.

They climb the stairs.

Good for us to walk. Need the exercise. Too many shortcuts.

Rendine can't recall entering the room. Doesn't remember sitting in the chair, Feels cold wire tape being stuck to his left temple and to the back of his head. Knows he is paralysed and it's not from fear.

Did you think I would let you win so easily, Rendine? Let's see you face fear now, with confrontation. See if your hypothesis works for you. The Games have never been the same since they let the Gallery decide. Second and third year students. What do they know?

Did I win then, Fergus?

No answer.

Rendine's heart beats faster. Fergus has not used Chloether but the old method of Transitional Transfer. Not so transitional this one. The mind is stuck until the operator removes the wires.

He's a sail on the river again. White, flowing, taking him to Fergus. They exchange their minds, occupy space behind each other's eyes. Join. No hiding, thoughts as transparent as ice. Two become one but stay divided.

Rendine feels fear like a dark cloak. Suffocating, dying, without the release.

Do you know that the body will try to give up if it passes the point of no return to living? How, then, can there be hope?

Tell me the story.

The last four words an echo mock.

They are alone. No one watching this time, no one to judge.

He thinks of the Hide and Go die syndrome, where the victim senses his demise and tries to hide from it, literally. Gets under the bed, behind cupboards, even under the carpet if it's loose.

No good, Rendine. Tell me the story.

A woman is having a baby. Her pelvis is too small for its head. She is alone. The baby is trying to be born. The pain is bad for her but unbearable for the child. After fighting to live, he begins to fight to die. He is trying to escape but can't. The worst fear of all. The woman's husband comes home and helps her deliver. The child feels fear the rest of its life but counteracts this with reckless behaviour. Some say he has a death wish. And so he does. It is the legacy of failure to die when he wanted to. But he lives on and accomplishes great things. Inspires others. Life – hope.

***

Mind pictures. Now Rendine is sinking in mountainous gaps. The light, blue intensive. The noise a buzzing vortex. Surrounded by an airless void.

He feels Fergus there with him, holding on. A mind-to-mind combat of the wills. He can't think of recourse. In this game, it seems, Fergus corners all the moves.

He wants to wake, struggles to rise but knows he cannot even as he is trying.

He skins his metaphoric knee. Feels the anger and cuts the perspective. The pull against him now like an undertow, fights it, wins by not giving ground. Needs just a moment's hiatus. Finds it and turns the picture absurd. Kangaroos walking. Horses hopping. Snakes in tutus. Fergus's mind withdraws like a sword leaving a scabbard.

Then Rendine hears a micromob; sounds like it's ringing underwater.

His eyes open to the living room. He sees only the ceiling fan turning slowly, corresponding with the wind-shifters on the roof to which it's joined.

He cannot move, can only just breathe. Has to concentrate to make his diaphragm lift, suck air in and out like bellows.

Fergus is talking to someone on his micromob. 'It's no good, I have to admit defeat. Yes, I have the Transvision… But you don't understand. He's done well in this too. Even under stress… Okay, come over. I need to see you too.'

Rendine sees Fergus slowly merge into vision. Hair hanging down. Looks younger than his fifty years.

'So,' Fergus says, 'back with us then?'

Those last words remind Rendine of Angela. He wishes it was her. Wonders if he will ever see her again.

He hears her voice. Thinks he may be imagining it. Then, when he hears it again, screams silently, Don't come closer, Ange. Go away, leave while you can.

Now he sees her face come into focus; her gilded hair touches his cheek. He is amazed how he can feel but not move.

She says nothing to him. Rendine is struck with a cold blow of realisation. She was the voice on the other end of the phone. She is in on this with Fergus.

Then he recalls how it was Angela who asked him out. Chose the cafeteria for them, where Fergus was waiting.

How could I have been so stupid? he thinks.

'If you are defeated, you will lose your a status as Master,' Angela is saying to Fergus. 'That could mean a transfer to another college. Not to mention a substantial cut in wages.' Her voice, honed granite.

Rendine sucks in air, concentrates on living. Wants to keep alive. Wants to level the score between them all.

Angela's face brushes over again. Non-committal eyes. Lashes half drawn.

'I just can't,' Fergus says. 'What you're asking… He'd be better off dead. And, Angela, listen, this guy's mind is wonderful. I can't deprive future generations…'

'Well, it's either me or him. That's my ultimatum, Fergus. Think what you'll lose, before you answer.'

Rendine hears the man sigh.

'I don't need to think. I only agreed to bring him here to do the mind-stress test, in case, like you said, he'd had outside help. But this stops right now. I'm bringing him back.'

Rendine feels relief lighter than summer; it's strengthened with the knowing that his hero worship of Fergus has not been misplaced. Then there's a fizz as the wire from the back of his neck is being removed. It catches on some hair and he winces inwardly but is glad of the pain.

He hears a knock on the door. Someone is walking across the room. When he finally sits up he sees that Angela is not Fergus's only visitor.

A man in a suit, with a fashionable triple tie, is giving Fergus his card. He glances at Rendine and nods. Then he holds out a hand to Fergus. 'I'm Adrian Jenson. Education Department, S.I. – Special Investigations. You've come up fine, by the way.'

Angela speaks up. 'Sorry about this, Fergus,' she says. 'There have been rumours. Nothing substantiated. But we had to make certain. Be sure about your integrity.'

Rendine sees that she is handing Fergus her card too. Over her shoulder, he reads Education Department, S.I., and Angela. Can't focus on her surname. Feels odd that he can only recall her first name.

She turns to Rendine. 'You did brilliantly, Ren. Oh shit,' she says. 'Adrian, have you got the Reversaclear? Of course, he doesn't remember.' She stops to help Adrian retrieve a slim tube of something from his briefcase. Then turns back to Rendine. 'We had to do that to you, Ren, make you forget certain things. If you had known, Fergus would have known.'

Adrian rubs pink gel, which smells faintly of pomegranate, on Rendine's arm. Rendine feels it travelling, a warm lava flow. Not unlike the first stage of getting drunk. But this clears his head. Recall floods like a tsunami. The picture of him volunteering to help check out Fergus Holinger fills his thoughts. God, that was a month ago, at least.

Then a warmer memory infuses him. 'Have you got my ring, Ange?' he says.

'Yeah,' she says.

Angela slips her hand in her pocket, retrieves a gold band identical to the one she's wearing on her ring finger, and slips it onto his.

The District Nurse Will Be Here Soon

The district nurse will be here soon.

I might ask her about me water. It's the same old trouble. Last time she just gave me some tablets and it went good.

I don't know why it happens, I keep meself warm enough. The red gum, he burns the best. Not like him bloody stringy bark. He's gone too quick, that fella.

And since I put down them pallets Joss brings with the apples, me feet don't get so dirty and I don't have to wash em every time I go to bed. It ain't healthy to wash too much.

The district nurse will be here soon.

I might ask her about me water.

When I go outside me shed this morning I'm straining like passing through the eye of a needle. I can't remember no more about that one. But they used to make us read from the Bible. I got a Bible once of me own when I read a whole verse. The tucker was good back then. But it's better here living in me shed.

The district nurse will be here soon.

I can never remember her name. She says to me, Mick, do you know who I am? I say, of course I do, missus, you come here every week. I know who you are. I likes you better than the other one. She never asks me anything, only tells me.

I'll say your name's Mary, and she'll say no, it's not, Mick, but where do I come from?

And I'll say Bunduburra and she'll laugh, and say, you always remember that, Mick.

Well, I'll say, I's right, ain't I? And she'll say, yes you are, Mick.

She doesn't know but I had a red kelpie pup called Mary. Lovely little bitch she was before the snake got her before I had all me cats.

Mary came from Bunduburra. I remember her colour, like the district nurse's hair. Red like this fire here.

It's a good fire. Red gum, he burns the best. Stringy bark, he's gone too quick that fella.

I think I will ask her about me water.

Men-o-stop

On a moonless evening there is no light; but me, I love the dark. My ex-husband says I have cat's eyes, in looks and ability. An unusual trait for a woman, he says. He always insisted on me driving at night. I never fail to spot the native fauna hell bent on beasticide, or dying to become roadkill. My night vision works just as well peripherally.

Darkness spreads ambiguity like a cosy blanket. Light casts a harsh reality, especially when you reach my age. My time of life.

Menopause.

My ex always used to joke that it should be called the men-o-stop, because he certainly wasn't getting it any more. He was expecting me to leave. Said he'd been treading the waters of anticipation (he could be a poetic bastard sometimes) waiting for me to walk out the door.

He had a lover waiting in the wings. I knew about her. I had my sources. Oddly enough, she hadn't been the reason for my final decision, but she certainly added straw to the already overburdened camel's back. If anything, she'd made it easier. Alleviated the guilt; although, really, he'd become like an adult child who refuses to leave home, and the only guilt I could have felt was that of maternal responsibility.

All of us are only a tiny gram of chemical away from insanity. Even the hormones the brain produces when you 'fall' in love can instigate a type of madness parodying OCD – obsessive compulsive disorder. My ex's favourite joke: how do you make a whore moan? I won't insult your intelligence with the answer.

I did try the patches, but I ended looking like a hostage survivor. One terrorists had stubbed their cigarettes out on. The tablets gave me some relief, until I woke to hysterical headlines of their dangers.

After going cold turkey, I reckoned the withdrawals I was suffering were much worse than any possible complications but my pay packet was a week away, and HRT is not for free.

That's why I was walking in the park that night.

I had made a rendezvous with my lover. Don't jump to conclusions; she was post-divorce and I'd only just discovered I was bi. Blame it on unbalanced hormones, I don't know. Anyway, I didn't think it could be any worse than being hetero. I'd found her on Internet Dating.

My son had warned me. 'Mum, only dropkicks or nutcases go on there.'

I think I knew which one was me.

Anyway, I was so damn miserable that in the heat of flush, or flash, as the Americans call it, I'd rung her and said I was finally ready to meet.

She was so excited, it reminded me of a puppy I had when I was a kid, although I hoped she wouldn't pee on me too.

As I hung up the phone, I pondered my rashness. But even the freezing night air was no match for my internal combustion and I could not bear another evening indoors. Funny what the body will drive you to do.

I suggested we meet in the park. It was central to us both.

We came from opposite sides of town – shades of Romeo and Juliet but on my current gender-bender I wasn't sure which I was meant to be – or not to be? I felt more confused than a hermaphrodite.

So there I was walking in the park, late at night, and dressed all in black, which was my recent mode of apparel. Menopause makes you put on weight and I was already three hundred pounds before it hit (black gives me, at best, a false sense of slimming, and at least hides the dirt).

It was an exceptionally dark night, the moon had waxed and was now in full wane, the stars hidden behind bruised purple clouds. I carried no torch. Like I said, I don't need one. Not with my cat's eyes.

I saw her in the distance, thirty feet away. She was right on time; I, as usual, was a couple of minutes late.

By courtesy of a flickering park light, which looked like it was going through some transitional, terminal stage too, I saw she was dressed all white and fluffy. Now she reminded me of a rabbit I once owned. I felt an instant attraction. No wonder people give their lovers 'pet' names – you know, like Kitten and Puppy. Right there I named her Bunny.

It was then I realised we were not alone. A man was scraping along the bushes, a torch pointed to the ground but his sights set determinedly ahead to where Bunny waited. A glint of a blade confirmed my fears. She hadn't seen him or me and I could see he didn't have my ability; even with a light he was stumbling.

I stopped breathing for a moment. Then anger kicked in. Here I was, finally feeling something, and then comes this guy wanting to jump the queue and snatch it from me. In the same instant I knew for sure. Me and Bunny – we were both Juliets. Men were antipathy not aspiration.

I also felt guilty. I should have met her in a bar or restaurant but I'd suggested we meet here because I'd been hoping the Doris Day lens of night light would soften the initial shock of my appearance. All it had done was put her life in peril.

I looked around for something I could use to level my chances. My ex used to say I was built like the back end of a front end loader, but this bastard still held the male advantage. And I swear on a stack of mothers, not three feet away was a cord. You know, the sort you use to secure stuff onto your bicycle.

Meanwhile, the prick was on top of Bunny and she was squealing like her namesake. Stupidly I scanned around, like her noise might attract other predators and then I leapt into action.

Jumping on the man's back, I felt the air knock out of him and her simultaneously. I hooked the rope around his neck and hung on like a demented rodeo rider; all that was missing were the spurs. I could see poor Bunny beneath us, a look of shock glazing her eyes.

What really surprised me was the quietness of it all; he didn't even grunt. But then I didn't give him a chance to air his vocal cords, the noose was twisted so tightly. Every rotten thing any bastard had ever done to me was momentarily and cathartically exonerated. The rush was greater than speed.

When he finally collapsed, Bunny humped him off with more strength than she looked to possess, and cast me a queried look of admiration.

I beat her to the intros. 'Hi, I'm Lexy,' I said, 'and you must be Bunny.'

She didn't argue with her new name. Why would she? I'd just saved her life. She only nodded and smiled in a lopsided way. I loved her instantly.

We dragged the body under the bushes and covered it with leaves. We figured that would give us some time before it was found. Already he had become an 'it'. Dehumanised. Although he'd done that long before we had.

Me, I wanted to go to the police. It was self-defence, after all. But Bunny shook her head when I suggested it. And, quite frankly, it was already a terrible start, without us spending our first evening together in some cop shop, having fingerprints taken and getting our mugshot. That light was even more unforgiving.

What else could I do but take her home? For the next several hours, over triple the number of glasses of wine, we learned more about each other than our husbands, or even our girlfriends, had ever known. Being partners in crime certainly lowers the benchmark of emotional inhibition. Bunny was a lot tougher than she appeared, and practical, so it wasn't long before we were laughing and joking, as if the evening had been some bad movie and we'd only watched the rerun.

Okay, eventually I did take her to my bedroom. No, I'm not going to divulge what happened. Let's just say it was the most fun I'd ever had, when I wasn't alone. And Bunny gave me a 'nick' that rhymed with Lexy. So I must have been pretty good too. She certainly lived up to her name.

From then on we were inseparable; talk about Siamese twins. Honestly, I felt I was reborn and this new HRT my doctor had put me on was great.

Then one evening, after watching the news about some poor old lady being raped and bashed to within a day of her four-score years and ten, we decided to do something. It was getting too damn crazy; this was the fourth assault we had heard of in as many days.

Surprisingly enough, it was Bunny's idea. 'Lexy,' she said, 'let me be a decoy.'

It didn't seem like a bad idea. The police weren't getting any closer to finding this pervert and we already had prior experience. Also, we seemed to have got away with it. No one had come round asking questions, and our incident was months ago.

I didn't agree straight away. It wasn't that I was squeamish; it was just I really loved Bunny, I truly did, still do, for that matter, and I was worried for her safety. But she kept badgering me, and when you love someone you want to make them happy.

After hearing about yet another rape and this time successful murder, in the same park where we'd met, I finally gave in. So began our night-time vigilante sessions.

I can tell you, it made it hard on my day job. But I managed to talk the boss into letting me do afternoon shift. That turned out to be perfect. Bunny would pick me up from work at midnight, we would drive to whatever park, and she'd walk her beat, as she called it. She made sure she didn't look like a pro, though. These degenerates usually want someone straight. It must add flavour to their excitement.

With my cat's vision, I was able to keep hidden while I followed the action. And the ligature I used was a little more sophisticated than the one I'd found on that first night. I'd made it shorter and tied a wooden bar to either end, which gave me better grip, and made it easier to deliver the *coup de grâce*.

You know, I can't understand it. Even now, I think me and Bunny should be getting a medal or something.

I know we shouldn't have taken the law into our own hands, literally. But really, we saved taxpayer money and freed up the police to do other things.

Yesterday, the rally outside supported us. They're calling us the

Serial-killer Killers. That made me happy. To know we have that support.

My trial comes up soon and my lawyer told me I should plead insanity. Tell me something I don't know, hey. And I'm not worried about Bunny, even though they haven't let us see each other (I suppose they think we may collaborate on our stories). Bunny's smart; she'll know what to say.

Yesterday my ex came to visit. He sat across from me for ages, shaking and nodding his head like one of those felt-flock dogs you see on the rear window of old people's cars. Finally he did speak, telling how he missed me – driving at night. Then he shifted sideways in his seat. 'Bloody hell, Lexy,' he said, 'you never do anything by halves. Other menopausal women just go up for shoplifting.'

What could I say? Even Bunny wouldn't have the answer to that one.

Broken Connections

Abby dips her toe in the bath like someone testing the water at the beach. But she does not stop, and plunges in with the rest of her body. The water smells of vinegar (her mother had told her it was the best disinfectant) and she glances at the empty bottle sitting on the floor. White brand from the supermarket. Everything she buys is on special or home brand. When there are eight to feed, it is a struggle to make any money stretch far enough.

The latest hit song echoes from her transistor radio like applause. *We shall overcome, we shall overcome…we shall overcome…someday…*

Abby shivers and lies back, sees her stomach, which is slightly swollen, sitting above the water like a tiny white island.

The water is so cold. The sort of cold you could only find down south. Like her mother would say when the tourists came for their warm winters in her home town of Leonora, Western Australia, 'Look at those people, off to the swimming pool and it's only twenty-five degrees. They must be from down south.'

When Abby met Brandon, one of those visitors from South Australia, and he told her his profession, she thought it was the most romantic thing she had ever heard. A lighthouse keeper. Such a noble calling. Saving all those people.

Now she hunches in the bath with her knees drawn up under her chin, arms wrapped around them in a sort of sitting foetal position. Immobilised. But she knows she has to move soon, make her arm reach out for her bag, the one with the paisley tapestry design, the one chattering with pins, needles, reels of cotton of every hue and all the buttons of her lifetime. Lost shirt buttons found long after the shirt had been made into rags. Buttons unpicked from babies' garments little more than dust cloths. Material covered buttons so big that she had let her children teethe on them. Everything has its use. Some have several. Her mother taught her that too.

Before running the bath and getting the vinegar from the pantry, Abby had waited until her youngest boy, Hamish, was tucked up in his cot. Everything normal. The same bedtime story: *The Very Hungry Caterpillar*. 'So much food he eats, mama.' Then the plaintive and predictable *I'm hungry*, so she'd gone to the kitchen, hoping she wouldn't wake any of the other five children while she looked for something she could bring him. She prayed Hamish would be asleep, and he was by the time she returned with a half cup of watered-down milk. Then she'd put her mind on hold, readying it for the final task of the evening.

They live so far from anywhere. A white stone cottage coupling with a lighthouse of the same construction, on an island outcrop. Twenty acres wide. And they have been 'working for the lights' for so long now that Abby has almost forgotten what before was like. The only other people living on the island are an old couple, inured and comfortable in their seclusion. They rarely socialise. Their only communication is a thin radio connection in predetermined hours. The operator on the mainland goes home after seven p.m.

Abby's husband, Brandon, is up in the tower. Checking, always checking. The light, with its many facets, has to be kept burning. The ships have to be saved. He is their lifeline.

Abby presses her lips together and leans forward in the icy bath. She grabs the bag of many buttons and it slips from her grasp. She is mildly grateful that it remains closed and the contents have not been spilled. She retrieves the bag and places it on her knees. With hands which do not feel like they belong to her, Abby takes out one of the large cloth-covered buttons and places it between her teeth. Then she reaches in and takes out what else she needs.

Now she is someone else. She recalls what her mother told her to do. Her fingers delve and open, and she tries, with the rug hook held tightly, to find the same pain she had felt when the doctor inserted that IUD four years ago. It had not worked. Hamish was born with it grown onto his wrist like a bracelet. He still bears the scar. But now, and she closes her eyes at this thought, it looks like a tiny question mark, whiter than his skin.

Abby clamps her teeth on the button. She feels the material slip a little, senses the structure of hardness beneath. Her jaw aches. With fingers stretching, she pushes against herself, feels something burst in a lightning of pain and then it is over and just beginning all at the same time.

She lies back and watches the red swirling from her as it warms the water. Her mother was wrong, she thinks distractedly; the cold water has not slowed the bleeding.

The batteries in her transistor seem to be fading, the voices like broken connections. But she sees the face of Brandon above her and, as if in a vacuum, she hears his cry. Now he is her lifeline.

Later she learns how he climbs the tower, flashes the light… three short, three long, three short…and thanks God that those he has saved so often are still familiar with the code.

Where the Truth Lies

When the gulls haunt the sea cliffs, dipping and climbing the wind like rising kites, and all the children of the houses that cling like periwinkles to the ledges above are tucked into bed three-apiece because that is all the comfort poverty will buy, a mother may tell in quiet words of the sea. What it gives and what it takes and sometimes what it leaves behind.

'Hush now, my little ones, and sleep will come to you. And Ellie, lie still too, while your father fights with the ocean to bring us back the fishy in the morning. We'll have work aplenty then with the salting and the pressing.' Her voice is soft, like the waves which froth in muted tones, curling the edged bed of the sea before hissing back to tuck the hidden depths.

And then Ellie, her eldest, says in plaintive pitch, 'Tell us again, Maither, tell us the story of the trousseau box.'

'Yes, yes,' Tommy and Marky, her two boys, clamour. 'Tell us about the pretty lady.'

And the mother sighs away the truth gnawing at her like the wave-eroded cliffs and begins her tale. 'It was not unlike a night as this, your father had not long gone a-sea, two nights before. Chasing the haddock he were. He were to be gone for three days more. And me alone, except for Ellie. But she had only seen four winters. The same as you two boys be now.' The mother pauses briefly. 'And me heavy with babe.' There is another short silence before she continues. 'I got up to the privy and then I saw a light.'

Then Ellie asks, 'Was it like the one Uncle Caleb sets up to guide in the ships?'

The mother gasps back a breath and pulls her shawl tightly around, her arms almost crossing herself. She doesn't answer, and bites her lip until the pain takes away the thought stinging her conscience like a wasp.

When she turns away her face, she finds her voice. 'The wind was so strong the grass was flattened like a mat and it blew me towards the cliffs. The shawl I had was not enough. I was in sore need of my coat. I hadn't got it on, the privy only being a little walk. So I came back for it.'

Suddenly the wind rattles the windows of shuttered wood then scurries up the cliff face to rustle the trees. The boys scrunch down in the bed until it seems that Ellie is its sole occupant but for the two little bumps merging to one.

The mother continues. 'The moon was high and washed like the rain had cleaned it. And I could see ahead without the use of a lamp. And the little light I had seen before was still a-twinkling. Then I heard a sound.'

'That were the pretty lady,' says Tommy, his voice blanket-muffled.

'Maither, tell Tommy to hush. Marky wants to hear it too.'

'Hush now,' says the mother, 'or I won't be telling it to any of you tonight.'

And so they are quiet while the mother tells of the pretty lady dressed in her finery lying on the sand and she as wet as the sea, and how the mother gave her coat to keep her warm. And how the lady kept asking for her trousseau box, saying how it contained much value. But how the candle in its silver holder, with its matching flint box, to light it, were the only things she took with her when the sailors came. And how she begged them to bring her trousseau box to the lifeboat, but they'd said it would mean they could save one soul less.

And when the mother draws a breath, Ellie slips from the bed, comes back holding a candle and lights it from the lamp. 'Look, Marky, this is not the candle but the holder is the very same, ain't it, Maither?'

And the mother nods and stares into the flame and goes as silent as the children have been until Tommy tugs her sleeve.

Then she finds her voice again. 'She was the most beautiful woman ever I'd seen. Hair she had like this flame.' The mother's breath makes the candle flicker until it almost goes out. 'And her skin was white and as fine as what they use at the courthouse to powder their wigs.'

'And the colour of her eyes, Maither, what about her eyes?' says Ellie, who does not let any of the story be forgotten.

'Ah, yes, the colour of her eyes.' The mother pauses again. 'They were green like the sea of a summer storm.'

Ellie jumps up again; the boys watch as she goes to the curtained cupboard below the stairs and comes back with a yellowing nightdress. There are threads hanging loose around its bodice and edges. 'This had real pearls on it, didn't it, Maither, until the sea took them?'

The mother takes the dress, lays it over her lap, strokes the silk.

She doesn't raise her eyes to her children until many are the minutes that pass. 'Ellie, you be putting back that candle now, do you hear? We don't have enough of them candles to be wasting.'

Her voice is sharp and the boys cover their heads once more with the old grey blanket, the one with the holes from the moths that let the cold in like tiny needles, and Ellie hurries the candle in its little silver holder back to the windowsill where it lives.

The mother keeps on stroking the nightdress, her fingers playing with the twisted knots, teasing up the threads and plucking at them like she would a chicken.

'I made to leave the lady then, because the cold was taking me. I was shivering so bad I said to her, I need to go now and can you walk a little way? Then we can shelter behind that crag over there. But the words she answered me tumbled about each other. Saying how she'd been married for but a year and her husband was waiting for her in their new home. Then she touched my arm and asked again about her trousseau box. Had I seen it and could I look for it. It were as if it were just a summer day and we'd mislaid a shoe on the way to the market. She said it in such a manner. Not panicked as she were but light and hopeful. I was scared then, as I'd seen others before her taken by a fever much less than hers.'

Marky stirs and gives a little cry, for the sleep that was teasing behind his lids with pictures of the pretty lady has vanished and all he has left is the hunger ache in his stomach and the cold tickling his toes like frost.

'She got to her feet and we walked towards shelter, where the wind was not as fierce. And she went to lie down before we were there so that

I had to hold her up. But I got her there and put the coat over her. She could go no more. When I came back the next morning she were gone and we never did find that trousseau box,' says the mother.

The boys are sleeping but Ellie sits as still as a wall, until her mother nudges her and tells her to climb back a-bed.

'And no more talk now. It's late and there'll be work for us all in the morning.'

The sea is stirring and grumbling like a drunken lover. The mother stares at the nightdress, hears the wind whispering, turns the pictures of the story around in her mind until they sit up straight and beg for the truth. The pictures become words of the lies she told her husband when he returned. How she delivered herself of two babes, not one, twin boys, and all on her own. Then she tells him of the lady, shows him the nightdress. But she has already washed the death-blood from its neckline and the birth-blood from its hem.

The contents of the trousseau box had bought them food and clothes for a year.

Later, the mother drapes the nightdress over a chair and goes to her own bed but she is not long there before she feels the blankets lift and Ellie slips in beside her like a fish.

She pulls the girl close and feels her arms encircle her. 'What is it, Ellie, can't you sleep, girl?'

'Maither,' says Ellie, her voice a notch above a whisper, 'I remember that night.'

'What do you remember?'

'You were not with babe when you went to the pretty lady, cause our Tommy had already come. Don't you remember, Maither? I got you the cloths and the knife to cut the cord. And Tommy had blood on him and he was screaming. But you said the screaming were good to made his lungs strong.'

'Why have you not told me all this before?'

Ellie shivers and turns over, stares at the ceiling. The stars are flickering light through the cracks in the roof.

'I seen other things that night that I don't understand, Maither. I need you to tell me.'

The mother sits up in bed. 'Tell me first what you saw.'

'When you came back for your coat, I followed you. But I kept back. I was scared then of the ghosts Uncle Caleb told me of. But now I know the ghosts is just a lie to scare people from finding the truth.'

'And what truth may that be, Ellie?'

'Uncle Caleb is a wrecker. Aint he, Maither? He murders people and takes what's theirs. I know that he puts out the lamps for the ships to come up on the reefs.'

Ellie's voice is loud and the mother snatches a glance at her two boys but they do not stir and for this she is glad.

The mother finds a memory of her own childhood, an awakening not unlike this night, but there was no pretty lady and all that she knew then was what her father and brother told her. It's the law, they'd said. If no one is found alive, then the owners of the shipwrecks will have no claim. They did not tell her of the part they played to make sure of no survivors, be they man or beast. They made a thin line between salvage and plunder, she thinks.

'Hush now, Ellie, or you'll be waking the boys. And don't tell your father any of this. He's a fisherman and proud of it. As most of the men in this village are. He knows of it all. And I don't visit with my family or my brother now.'

'You lie.' Ellie spits the words like a snake.

The mother raises her hand but then her arm falls limp to the bed. 'Oh, Ellie, I cannot abide this. What did you see?'

'I seen you and Uncle Caleb. But that were later. Earlier you came back for the knife, the same knife I'd brought to you only a few sleeps before that day. When our Tommy was born.'

The mother takes Ellie into her arms, and whispers. 'Oh, my poor lamb, you should not have seen it.' She sits up in bed and pulls her shawl around her shoulders. 'The pretty lady was with babe and it was coming and would wait for no one. That's why she could not walk. She was brave and I helped as I could. She was torn between this world and the other.'

Ellie is snuggling into her mother's side.

The mother brushes away a strand of Ellie's hair. 'I kept thinking this is what my Ellie saw when Tommy came. Oh, and it is so beautiful, such a wonder. I took the babe to the pretty lady's breast. And how strong the babe were, Ellie. How it suckled. And its maither, her face were so soft it were like the silk of her nightdress. And her smile it were sunshine. I wrapped the babe in this shawl.' The mother touches her shawl with a fingertip caress. 'So I had only my dress. But I didn't feel cold. The wind went away and the night went still. And that's no lie, Ellie. I swear. Then the pretty lady were thanking me. Thanking me, Ellie! Me, a lowly fisherman's wife and she so highborn. Oh, that moment I wished would never go.'

'But then Uncle Caleb came, didn't he, Maither? Why was he angry? I got so scared, I ran home.'

The mother sighs a long breath. She hugs Ellie and lies back on the pillow. She feels relieved that the child did not see what happened next.

Before she could stop him with word or action, her brother had taken the knife and run the blade across the pretty lady's throat. A thin line. She had not made a sound and her eyes staring, green like the sea of a summer storm, were the last thing the mother remembers of her before snatching up the babe.

She told her brother that if he tried to take the babe from her she would tell her husband, when he returned from the sea. 'Not if you're dead, you won't,' her brother had said. But then laughter followed in her wake as she fled, and the words, 'You'll both stay safe enough if you keep quiet.'

Ellie says, 'Maither, Marky belongs to the pretty lady, doesn't he?'

'No, Ellie child, not now he doesn't. He's mine, and he's your brother and Tommy's twin. You must remember this truth and say no other.'

Ellie is silent and lies back to sleep.

The mother thinks of the trousseau box, carved oak, how she found it the next day, wedged in a cove, seaweed like sirens' tresses wrapping it hidden. She kept it secret from her husband. And what it held saved them all the following year when the fish did not come and when the winter was so harsh the boats could not go out even if they had.

The mother climbs from the bed, takes the nightdress from the chair and draws back the tattered curtain where an open wooden box, without its lid, stands on its side for a cupboard. She stares at the square oak plates, their backs ornately carved but their edges roughly cut, the knife pared by years of sharpening to a thin line.

A draught flutters the curtain and she thinks she needs to be putting more tallow between the cracks once again, come a pleasanter day.